Sleep Well,
Baby Girl, and Dream

Written by
Lora E. Sandler

Illustrated by
Kelley Boggio

All thanks and praise to God,
our creator.

To my two baby girls who I love dearly, and
who have been living their dreams.

And to my precious mother who fell
(and who has recovered wonderfully well!).

~ Lora E. Sandler

Sleep Well,
Baby Girl, and Dream

A mama came home with

her dear baby girl,

not long after bringing her into

this big, bright world.

Baby Girl cried

and Mama sighed,

and she thought of

what she should say.

Because sometimes the world felt so big.

And sometimes the mama felt small.

There were times when she knew just what to do.

And times she had no idea at all.

She held Baby Girl

and gave her a kiss.

Then the mama would say to her

sweet, sleepy miss...

Sleep well, Baby Girl, and dream.

Dream of how you are growing.

Dream of what you are learning.

Dream of the people you'll meet,

and the places you'll see.

Dream of love, joy, and peace.

Dream of the wonderful girl

who I know you to be.

Baby Girl grew and

began to walk, talk, and run.

She loved to meet people

and she loved to have fun.

She would finish her days

in her mama's safe arms.

Because sometimes things seemed
too hard to do.

And sometimes Baby Girl felt okay.

There were times when she
easily listened.

And times she just wouldn't obey.

But after a story, a kiss, and

a bedtime prayer,

the mama would say as she stroked

her baby girl's hair...

Sleep well, Baby Girl, and dream.

Dream of how you are growing.

Dream of what you are learning.

Dream of the people you'll meet,

and the places you'll see.

Dream of love, joy, and peace.

Dream of the wonderful girl

who I know you to be.

Baby Girl started school

and learned things great and small.

She studied and practiced

and she grew so tall.

At the end of each day

she raced home all the way

to tell her dear mama about it all.

Because sometimes the work

was confusing.

And sometimes she learned so well.

There were times she could do things

all by herself.

And times when she needed some help.

But at bedtime her mama would

snuggle her close.

And Mama would say the words Baby Girl loved

the most...

Sleep well, Baby Girl, and dream.

Dream of how you are growing.

Dream of what you are learning.

Dream of the people you'll meet,

and the places you'll see.

Dream of love, joy, and peace.

Dream of the wonderful girl

who I know you to be.

Baby Girl went off

and away on her own.

She met so many new people

and put their names in her phone!

She traveled and visited and saw

interesting places.

She took pictures and made memories

with so many new faces!

As she laughed and she smiled,

she thought of Mama at home.

Yet even with friends, Baby Girl felt alone.

Because sometimes her life was so complicated,

And sometimes it all made sense.

But lots of times Baby Girl needed guidance.

And calling Mama was her best defense!

So sometimes at night,

when things didn't seem right,

Baby Girl would make the call,

and Mama's words said it all...

Sleep well, Baby Girl, and dream.

Dream of how you are growing.

Dream of what you are learning.

Dream of the people you'll meet,

and the places you'll see.

Dream of love, joy, and peace.

Dream of the wonderful girl

who I know you to be.

And then the day came,

Baby Girl changed her name!

She married the man who she loved!

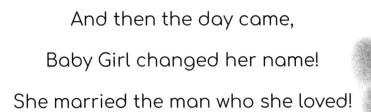

They both worked so hard

in their home and at their jobs.

And their peace, love and joy

Brought forth a sweet baby boy!

Because sometimes the world

felt so big.

And sometimes Baby Girl felt small.

There were times when she knew

just what to do.

And times she had no idea at all.

When she heard Mama's voice

on the end of the line,

Baby Girl always knew

that it all would be fine...

Sleep well, Baby Girl, and dream.

Dream of how you are growing.

Dream of what you are learning.

Dream of the people you'll meet,

and the places you'll see.

Dream of love, joy, and peace.

Dream of the wonderful girl

who I know you to be.

And then came a day

when Mama's hair was gray,

and Baby Girl got a terrible call.

Mama had taken a fall!

She wasn't well at all.

Could Baby Girl come right away?

And this big, grown-up girl

knew she had to be strong,

for the mama who loved her and

helped her for so long.

She climbed into the bed and stroked

Mama's sweet head.

This time nothing seemed right

so she held Mama tight.

And Big, Grown-Up Girl sang soft,

peaceful songs and whispered sweet

words in Mama's ear.

She breathed in really deep,

and to help Mama sleep,

said the words she knew Mama could hear...

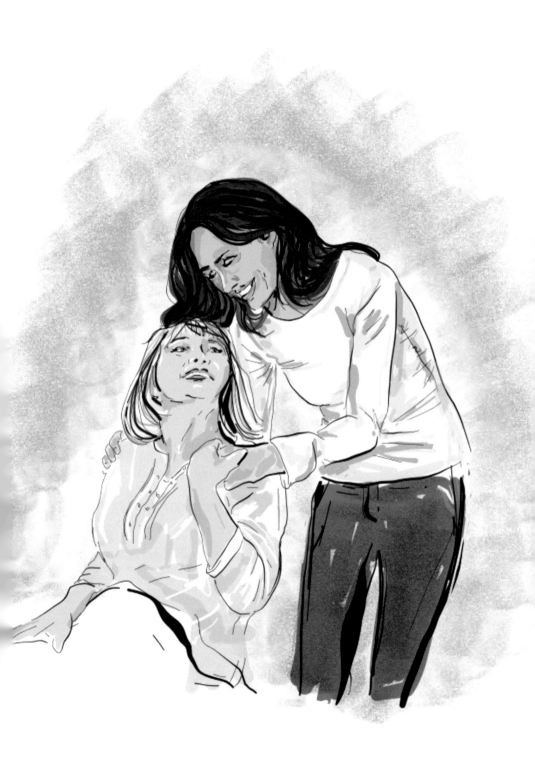

Sleep well, Mama dear, and dream.

Dream of how I am growing.

Dream of what I am learning.

Dream of the people I'll meet,

and the places I'll see.

Dream of love, joy, and peace.

Dream of the wonderful girl

who you raised me to be.

And Big, Grown-Up Girl cried

and sweet Mama sighed.

They hugged and they smiled until

Mama got tired.

And Mama dreamed all the dreams

of her precious girl,

and the fine things she had done

in this great big world,

and the people she met,

and the places she went,

and how wonderfully she grew,

and how much she knew.

And Mama slept with a heart full of

love, joy, and peace.

Lora E. Sandler is a gifted author, teacher, and Registered Nurse who resides near Atlanta, Georgia.

There she uses her talents in many venues including teaching piano and Spanish, cooking gourmet meals, enjoying the outdoors, gardening, and writing both chapter books (one is in the editing process right now!) and illustrated books for children.

Her illustrated children's book, The Girl with Caterpillars in Her Hair, is available for purchase on Amazon.

Lora is also active in her community and in her church.
She and her husband of 37 years have five grown children and six grandchildren (with, hopefully, many more in the future). Much of her inspiration comes from the wonderful antics of her charming family.

Lora enjoys speaking about writing at schools and to adult groups. Please send her a message if you would like to schedule a speaking engagement.

She also makes many appearance at vendor events.
If you see her, please stop by so she can meet you and sign your book. You can learn more about her and send her messages at:
Lora E. Sandler Author on Facebook.

Please take a moment to rate this book on Amazon.
Lora reads and appreciates every written review!

If you're looking for the "boy" counterpart for this story, it will be starting production in 2023!

Kelley S. Boggio is an accomplished designer, illustrator and fine artist who is recently married and now lives in Calera, Alabama.

Named "Kiki" by all the little ones in her family and with a new surge of painting inspiration - Kiki Motif was born.

Botanicals and people were the first subject matter of inspiration in her life and have never lost their luster. Her work has expanded from fine art to using art in design. Clients from interior decor stores, large department stores, concept car design groups, and more have embraced her textural style, eye for whimsy, and use of negative space.

The collection of illlustrations before you are a culmination of Kelley's love for family, a friend's vision, and for a fellow sister in Christ.

If you'd like to see more of her work check out her site kikimotif.com!

Made in the USA
Columbia, SC
27 August 2024

41228563R00038